MUNCH

Written and
illustrated by
Emma McCann

little bee

The alarm clock went off...

DRING! DRING!

...just as MUNCH was enjoying a very nice dream about toast and coconut jam.

Dragging himself out of bed, he went to the kitchen to have breakfast.

He was just munching his way through his 17 slices of toast with banana jam, when something caught his eye in the newspaper.

GIANT MONSTER GOES RAVENOUS RAMPA

This picture taken by a reader some fear to be the enormous

An enormous monster caused chaos in Wibble town centre yesterday as it ate its way through hundreds of houses. Terrified homeowners watched in horror as the huge creature swallowed down several streets, leaving many monsters homeless, before

crunch
cars fo
Nobc
plan
com
has
pla
fea
st
v

"GOOD GRIEF!" exclaimed MUNCH out loud, dropping his toast on the floor. "Maybe I should stay home and protect my house from being eaten!"

MUNCH sat up all day,

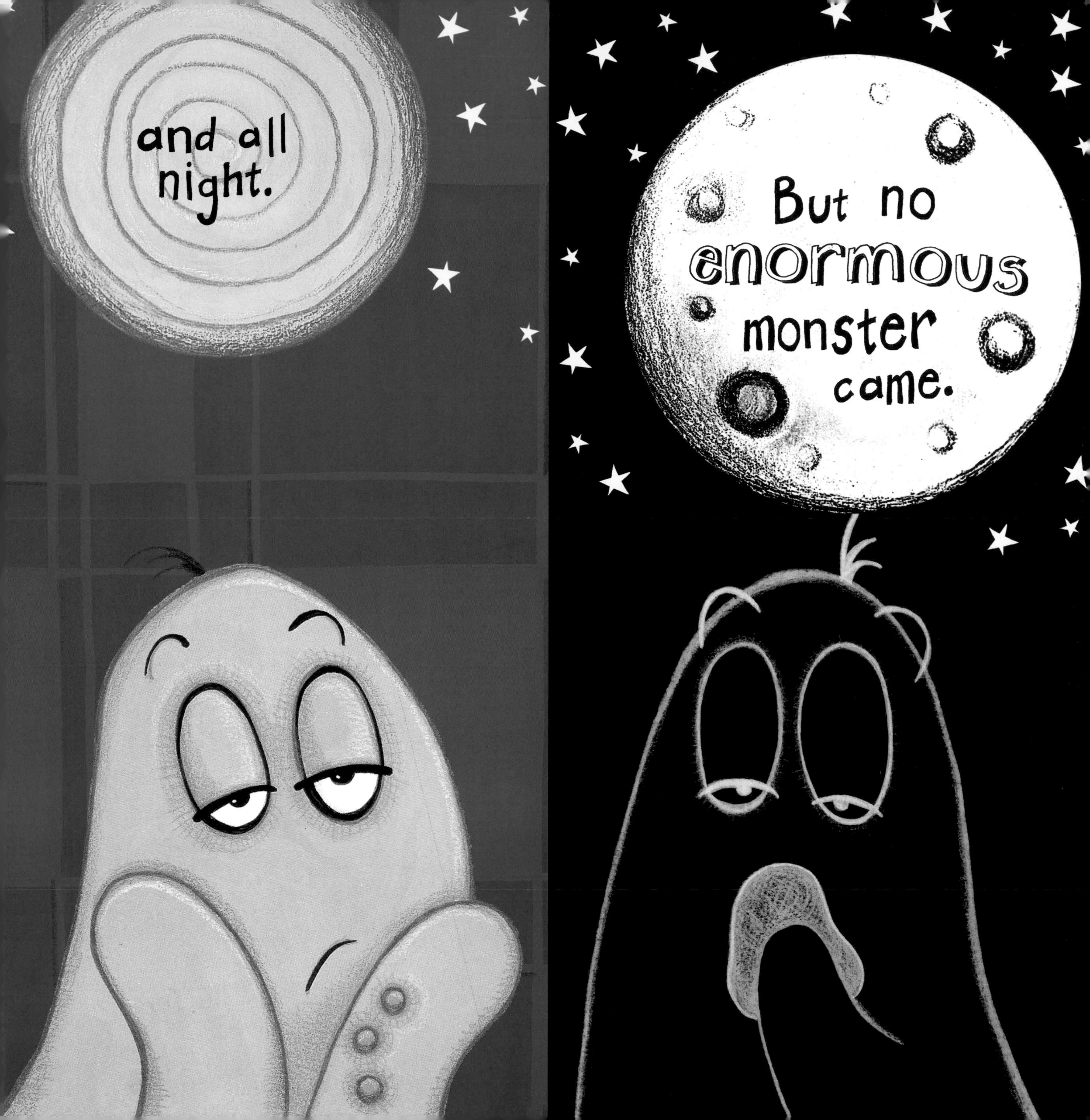
and all night.
But no enormous monster came.

The same evening over **11** slices of toast with broccoli jam, MUNCH put on the television.

The news was on and something caught his eye.

The **enormous** monster that MUNCH had seen in the newspaper was on the television gulping down **trees** and **lamposts** and buses and anything else it could fit in its gigantic mouth.

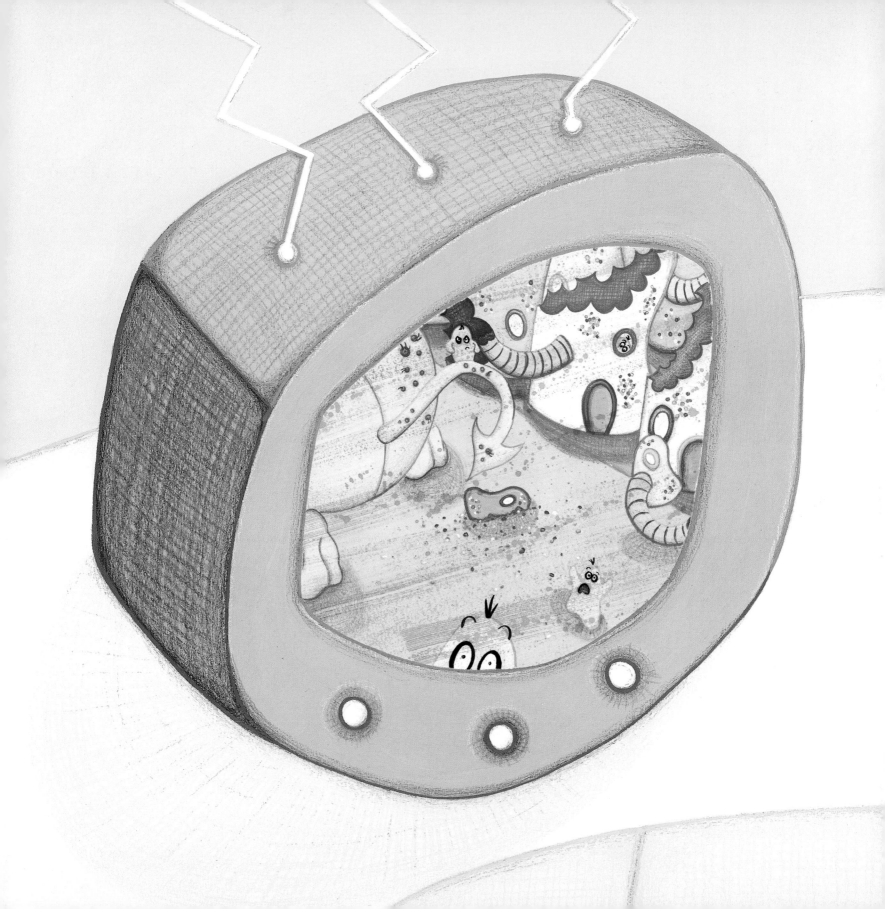

and all day.

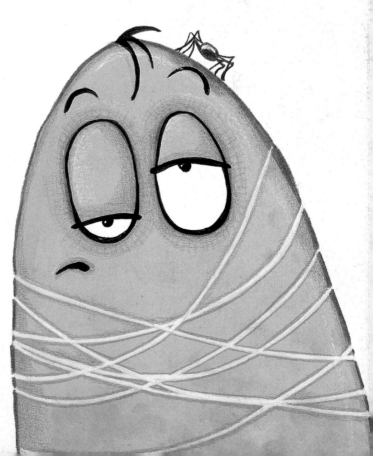

But no enormous monster came.

The next morning MUNCH went to make toast and jam as usual but something wasn't quite right!

"Where's my television?"

"Where's my fridge?"

They were definitely there yesterday.

Then MUNCH noticed the worst thing of all...

He marched outside
slamming the door,
and came face
to face
with...

The **enormous** monster!

"OI!" he shouted. "You've eaten my jam!"

The **enormous** monster looked all around to see where the little voice was coming from.

It saw MUNCH'S
angry face and
started to laugh.

And the more it laughed,
the angrier MUNCH became.

The enormous monster
came closer and closer
licking its lips.

It bent down,

opened its mouth and...

MUNCH swallowed him up instead.

Pity he had no jam.

For Muvver and Spud
E.M.

Even if one prefers lemon curd and the other doesn't like toast.

First published in 2005 by Meadowside Children's Books
185 Fleet Street, London, EC4A 2HS.
This edition published 2006 by Little Bee,
an imprint of Meadowside Children's Books

The right of Emma McCann to be identified as the
author and illustrator of this work have been
asserted by her in accordance with the Copyright,
Designs and Patents Act, 1988.
A CIP catalogue record for this book
is available from the British Library.
Printed in Indonesia
10 9 8 7 6 5 4 3